SPRING AT THE BOW-TIQUE

Written by **Allison Grote**

Illustrated by **Loter, Inc.**

D𝒾sney PRESS

LOS ANGELES • NEW YORK

Minnie loves spring.

Minnie sells spring clothes.

The girls come in.

"Try this," says Minnie.

They like it!

Good job, Minnie.

Penelope Poodle
comes in.

"Try this," says Minnie.

Penelope likes it!

Good job, Minnie.

Mickey comes in.

"Try this," says Minnie.

He likes it!

Good job, Minnie.

Clarabelle comes in.

"Try this," says Minnie.

Clarabelle does not like
spring clothes.

"I like my bow better,"
says Clarabelle.

"Try this," says Minnie.
"Or this!"

"I like my bow better,"
says Clarabelle.

"Try this," says Minnie.

"I like my bow better,"
says Clarabelle.

Clarabelle sits.

Minnie thinks.

Bows!

More bows are better!

"Try this!" says Minnie.

"Or this!" says Minnie.
Clarabelle loves it!
Good job, Minnie.

Penelope yells,
"I like her bows better!"

Penelope waits.

She loves it!
Good job, Minnie.

They love spring!